Tule Fog Wary:
Tule fog

Vincent R. Petrucci

Tule Fog Wary: Tule Fog

© 2022 Vincent R. Petrucci

ISBN:
Paperback   979-8-88615-067-4
E-Book   979-8-88615-068-1

Inks and Bindings
888-290-5218
www.inksandbindings.com
orders@inksandbindings.com

CONTENTS

The book is dedicated to

My wonderful and loving Parents

Dino Antonio Petrucci and Peggy Louise Petrucci

I want to give special thanks to Edgar Ruiz for all the illustrations and book cover.

TULE FOG WARY

The day appeared to be somewhat like the morning. Tule fog was thick, the sun had not come out in over 3 weeks in the valley where Lorenzo lived, just a blanket of white cold and misty air.

A typical January day. Lorenzo was out on the tractor shredding the vineyards, lots of brush from prunings. The tractor had a small barrier on the back side, this prevented the flying pieces of wood from hitting Lorenzo's ears and head, yet there were still times that the wood inflicted pain to the back of Lorenzo's body.

Lorenzo's uncle would tell him to wear these goggles. He bought them at a sale out in Chowchilla last Thursday. That sale, wow, his uncle loved that sale. To Lorenzo, it was with lots of junk yet his family like that and do not turn around just watch the row in front of you. Lorenzo looked at the protective equipment and thought... Wow, these look like something his Nonno had brought from Italy many years ago. This was not Lorenzo's favorite job, shredding the vineyard, yet he was earning money and enjoyed working in the fresh air.

Lorenzo, 21 years old, had finished high school and was working on his family's farm. His daily tasks consisted of pruning vines, to feeding cows and sheep. Today, he was shredding the vineyard with an old shredder and an AC tractor that was running well this afternoon. The fog again today has not lifted, looks like the day into the night with the same weather.

The rain had come last week allowing the fog to form,it was cold and wet. It felt just like rain, a heavy spray, they call this tule fog. It was named from the tule plant which grows in low wet lands around this valley. Lorenzo's father always reminded him, never drive fast in the tule fog, it's deadly. It has caused a lot of car accidents. Always have your windows down and do not get too comfortable driving in tule fog… it really did not bother Lorenzo. He would just take a few hits from that nice mean green and get into driving the tractor. There was no cab. It was open air. Lorenzo had on winter gear, yet it was still cold.

FRESH AIR

It was boring driving that tractor, yet Lorenzo had his dogs running with him all day. They kept him entertained chasing rabbits and or retrieving birds that Lorenzo would shoot from the tractor with his 20 gauge pump. Most of the birds were starling birds and or crows, rabbits, etc. During pheasant season, Lorenzo would shoot ringnecks and also enjoyed dove hunting during the season. Never shoot the hawks. It was illegal. Lorenzo's father had taught him to follow the law when it came to hunting. He stated fines from the game warden were high, and they could take away your gun. At times, Lorenzo's Nonno would shoot the chicken hawks that were preying on hens around the farm.

Lorenzo respected his Nonno. He was an intelligent man, not so tall yet had huge arms and hands. He knew how to do just about anything from building livestock corrals, to making blood sausage. Vincenzo, his Nonno, was an independent man. He had plenty of friends that would come over and half a half glass of wine and talk.

One particular friend was Angelo. Lorenzo's Nonno liked Angelo. He was a painter. Vincenzo would say in Italian, "Here comes Angelo the *pittore*!" Lorenzo recalls going to Angelo's home in the small town and eating homemade soup from fresh tomatoes, such a treat. Vincenzo was an acquaintance of Angelo, who was an excellent painter, something Vincenzo was not. Lorenzo loved visiting Angelo. Lorenzo heard through his cousin that Angelo was involved. Lorenzo never really knew what it meant. Angelo was a kind man, short with thinning hair and an odd smile. Lorenzo found out later that Angelo was gone. He never came over to the farm again.

LIVESTOCK

During those cold winter nights of the thick tule fog, the lights were on in the corrals. Lorenzo's father raised sheep, this was a deterrent to the dogs and coyotes that would come in and attack the ewes and lambs. Lorenzo knew if the lamb had been eaten or partially consumed it was a coyote, yet if the animal was just dead, then it had been a dog. The dogs chased the ewes until they died of exhaustion. It was terrible and a bit scary to hear the howling of the coyotes after killing a small lamb. That eerie cry was frightening..

Shot guns out near the barn were loaded with easy access to protect the animals. Lorenzo had killed some coyotes and dogs that had caused a great amount of damage to the sheep.

There was also a gun safe in the house, Lorenzo's mother had bought this for Lorenzo's father for Christmas. Some shot guns were leaning in the corners of the house. Not the best practice yet easy to retrieve. This was 1967, safety measures were up to each family.

This was legal. If a stray dog and or other predator was killing your livestock, the law states you have the right to defend your stock. In fact, one of Lorenzo's dogs had been killed, an American Pit Bull Terrier. Lorenzo had found the dog on the side of the road as a puppy along with his brother. One dog was pure white. Lorenzo named him Cain, the other brown his name was Pepper. Lorenzo could never keep those dogs out of trouble. One day, the neighbor came from down the road. He was a different type of man. Never said much, yet the family knew his in-laws. "I killed your white dog, Lorenzo, he killed my barbado sheep," the strange looking man stated.

Lorenzo walked over to the neighbors pasture, where his dog, Cain, was covered in blood. Lorenzo picked up his dog, took him to his family's property and buried him. Lorenzo was sad, yet knew what the law was. He accepted what the strange looking man had done, however, Lorenzo never really liked him until the present day. In the back of Lorenzo's mind, the strange looking man was jealous of Lorenzo and his dogs that were with Lorenzo each day out on the tractor.

Lorenzo was only 21, yet knew all about guns. Cleaning them, taking them apart, and he especially knew that they were dangerous and could kill. "Guns were used to hunt or to protect our animals," Lorenzo's father had taught him. Never ever point a gun at any person, even a play gun; this was a strict rule of his father, which Lorenzo always followed. He listened to his father and loved him very much.

Lorenzo's father was an avid hunter, he would tell him stories as a young boy going out and killing gunny sacks full of birds. Lorenzo's father had bought him a Daisy BB gun when he was 8 years old. Lorenzo remembers when he himself went through the hunters safety course. He passed the exam and was able to hunt when seasons were open. All Lorenzo's friends were taking the class. Most of his friends had small and or larger farms and were hunters.

His father would put stick matches in the dirt and teach Lorenzo to shoot the head off the match stick from 20 feet away. Lorenzo had a good aim and was precise in his shooting, yet always respected the guns and cared for them.

It was near 4 pm. The sun was almost down. Night was upon us and the fog was coming in thicker than last night. Lorenzo was ready to take the tractor into the shed.

SHORT DAYS

The howling of the coyotes had already started. The sound echoed through the vineyard rows. Winter days were short. The sun was down near 4:30 in the afternoon yet with the fog even at 3:30 pm, it appeared dark. Lorenzo's father had just arrived from the *rancho grande*, which was located 11 miles north of Lorenzo's home. He mentioned to go out and check the new born lambs, one white faced mother had twins. They were strong and already sucking well off their mother, yet take a look at them.

"Come on, Blood," Lorenzo calls his dog and they walk through the pasture checking the ewes. "Let's take this one into the barn," Blood was happy and followed every step of Lorenzo. This ewe was near lambing giving birth, Lorenzo did not want to leave a weak mother out in the thick fog tonight. This was too easy prey for the predators...

"Look, blood," Lorenzo pointed to the mushrooms that were growing in the pasture. These come out in the cold misty foggy winter days. Lorenzo had gathered plenty of mushrooms in the past with his Nonno and Nonna yet was not an expert. Lorenzo knew mushrooms were poisonous, and only certain types were good to consume. He would leave mushroom gathering to his Nonno and Nonna.

"When they are with me, Blood, we can pick them," Lorenzo told his dog.

Lorenzo, who was brought up on the farm, enjoyed caring for and raising sheep. He, along with his sister Fylnn, entered the sheep in a few fairs around the valley. Fylnn had won grand champion at some big fairs in San Francisco a few different times. Lorenzo also had trophies. Lorenzo told his dog, "I love these sheep, Blood, they are like my family. Dad wants us to make sure all is safe," Lorenzo's dog would shake and wag his tail. His dog was a loyal friend to Lorenzo, always happy. Blood was part of the family and would never betray Lorenzo. He was a huge black Great Dane. Blood loved to chase rabbits, and Lorenzo enjoyed watching him run.

EARLY RISER

The next morning, up early and feeding the sheep, Lorenzo noticed a ewe down. She had fallen over. It appeared she was trying to lamb deliver her baby. Blood was there barking. Lorenzo took off his coat quickly and rolled up his sleeve. There was ice on the ground and very foggy, he put his hand into the vaginal track of the ewe and delivered the baby lamb. "Wow," Lorenzo yelled, "We saved the mother and the lamb, Blood. You see, Blood," Lorenzo said to his dog.

Sometimes, the mother being so fat with newborns ready to deliver, needs help. If we would not have seen her she could have died. Lorenzo's father always encouraged him to check the animals each day and night. He would say, "If you have something, take care of it, Lorenzo. Feed them, water them, manage them."

"We were at the right place and at the right time, Blood," he told his dog.

The southwest side of the farm was on the opposite side of the county road, there was a small pasture that the sheep also grazed on. It was winter, not much for the sheep to eat, yet Lorenzo would take over alfalfa hay to satisfy them. The sheep would cross into the next pasture underneath the road.

There was a large old irrigation pipe. It was big enough to walk through if a person was bending over. The sheep did not like to pass through this tunnel, yet Lorenzo would take buckets of grain to entice them. The sheep would follow.

Lorenzo himself really did not like crawling under that old cement irrigation pipe,yet it provided a safe aveune for the animals to cross the road. It was dark and Lorenzo recalls his Nonno saying, stay alert when moving the sheep underneath the road. There are a lot of black widow spiders and wasp nests inside the old pipe.

Lorenzo would watch his father go into the pipe with a paper lit on fire and burn out the angry wasps. It was cold now, so the wasps would not be around yet Lorenzo was wary. "Come on, Blood," Lorenzo said to his dog, "Let's cross over and bring in the sheep."

Lorenzo's dog was barking. "What's the matter?" Lorenzo gestured to the dog. As Lorenzo walked forward, he saw some eyes piercing at him in the dark tunnel. Suddenly, the eyes came toward Lorenzo, Blood was moving toward the creature. "Wow, it's a red fox," Lorenzo yelled. The fox darted out of the irrigation pipe. Blood was closing in, however the fox was too quick and jumped the fence. Blood stood there barking disappointed…

"My gosh," Lorenzo stated, "that was a shock… It really startled me, Blood…"

DIFFERENT ROLE

That night, Lorenzo's family had a party to cater the event that would start at 7 pm. Lorenzo's father had been preparing the meal throughout the day with a few of the farm's employees.

The catering business was like a hobby for Lorenzo's father, he enjoyed the time to socialize. He had started the business a few years ago. He was a determined man that was not afraid to work. He liked people, furthermore would make a few pennies. He would tell Lorenzo, "We can do anything, Lorenzo. It does not make a difference what you do. Work hard and respect others." Lorenzo's father had vision and lots of desire.

Tonight, it was for a family's mother, her 90th birthday. Around 60 people served ceramic plates through a buffet line. His specialty, tri-tip beef with all the fixing. Chili beans, scalloped potatoes, fresh garden salad, and fruit. Lorenzo recalls there were 6 of us that night serving in our white smocks. Lorenzo's father served a good meal and his staff was always sharp and ready to work.

Lorenzo enjoyed working alongside his family. Lorenzo had not gone to college, this was his job. Happy to be off the tractor, assisting with catering. Lorenzo liked farming, yet out on that tractor was cold and lonely at times. So catering, it was fun and he's able to venture out, with lots of fringe benefits, the girls at the parties.

NIGHTMARE

It was 9 pm, he was driving home from serving the party, tule fog, thick, cold, wind blowing as he was driving home in the catering van, able to only see 2 yellow lines in front of him. The mist was heavy. Lorenzo was using his windshield wipers and was driving slowly with his windows down, following his father home. In a split second, there was a car in the same lane coming head on. Frank, one of the employees, yelled *watch out* in spanish to Lorenzo. The van veered off the road and nearly hit a tree. Lorenzo had avoided a terrible accident. Still in shock, Lorenzo made it back to the farm safely, yet was really shaken up. His heart was still racing.

Lorenzo unloaded the van with Frankie. "I am going to bed. It's been a long day and your mother is not feeling well." Lorenzo gestured to his father, "I will finish up, Dad." Lorenzo did not mention the near-fatal accident to his father.

Lorenzo lived across the farm in his grandparents' old house. It was a 3-minute drive down the 1/2 mile dirt road. He could hear his dogs barking in the distance. Lorenzo was married and had a 2-year-old son. His wife was home waiting for him. She was a sweet, kind person who was always positive. Lorenzo loved her and was a good friend with his wife, Jerry Ann. Lorenzo would always say that myself and my wife agree on politics and music...

Upon arrival, his wife cheerfully greeted him, "How did it go Lorenzo?"

"All was well, yet almost got hit head on. A car was in my lane coming fast. Frank yelled and I was able to get to the side of the road. Killer tule fog. So bad. My father, oh wow same old self. Forgot knives at the kitchen, so I had to drive back home in this terrible fog."

"Are you okay?" Lorenzo's wife asked him. He replied, "Yes, I am. How is Santo?" Santo is Lorenzo's son. "He is sleeping," his wife stated.

I made it back on time. The party was a success as it seemed to always be. Lorenzo's father had started his catering business some 3 years ago. He was a teacher, farmer and now was going to take on the food business. So far, it was going okay. Lots of work with a small amount of profit.

Lorenzo's mother would always be complaining, "Your father is doing what he wants, yet not making money."

You see, Lorenzo's parents were always engaged in the community, social folks. They donated a lot of time. They were good people… Lorenzo's father loved to stay busy, was involved in the service clubs, Lions Club, 20/30 Club, Little League Baseball, Babe Ruth Baseball, 4h Club and FFA, Future Farmers Of America. He loved FFA. Lorenzo's father was also an FFA member and had won a national public speaking contest when he was in high school years before. They would transport team mates home from games when their parents did not show up. They would support charities. They would raise money from the catering business and donate to the event.

Lorenzo's parents were kind, giving and caring. Lorenzo loved his family.

UNTHINKABLE...

Lorenzo will never forget that phone call that changed his life, as well as his entire family's life on the cold foggy windy night to the present day.

"Lorenzo, get up! Something terrible had happened," They had knocked down the door at Lorenzo's parents house. "Who? What happened?" Lorenzo demanded of his sister, Flynn. "They were disguised as police," Flynn stated

Lorenzo arrives at his mother and fathers home. The dogs are barking nonstop. There were so many red lights from the sheriff's department.

Lorenzo first thought his mother was ill. She had just had surgery on her hip. Her health was poor, yet seemed to have been healing in recent days.

The officer approached Lorenzo. "Your parents have been victims of a home invasion," he stated. "The fog was so thick, we were unable to track the perpetrators. Never seen tule fog so bad," stated one of the sheriff officers

Lorenzo ran into the house. His mother was bleeding from her nose. She was upset, yet as always, was strong. "I am okay, Lorenzo. Where is your father?" She was crying and worried, Lorenzo felt terrible seeing his mother in this condition, imagine you were in deep sleep and some loser low-life breaks into your home… *My poor innocent mother,* Lorenzo thought.

The kitchen floor and cabinets were covered in blood. Lorenzo's father was seated in the living room next to the fireplace. There, Flynn was trying to comfort him. There must've been 10 sheriff officers in the home.

"They came to the door, Lorenzo, knocking nonstop," Lorenzo's father stated. "Next, I remember I was in the kitchen. I tried to find the gun. I could not see they had knocked my glasses off. They kept demanding money. 'Where is the safe?' one said," Lorenzo's father was trying to explain, yet he also was covered in blood, both eyes swollen. He was grimacing with pain and holding his ribs from the beating he endured, they had tied him with duct tape and threw him into the swimming pool.

Flynn, Lorenzo's sister, stated, "My dogs were going crazy. I thought there were coyotes in the pasture, yet could not see 5 feet in front of me because of the thick tule fog."

Flynn, who lived on the south east end of the farm, rushed over to find Lorenzo's father bobbing in the swimming pool. Flynn had saved him… his hands had been duct taped behind his back. Flynns dogs were the heroes. Her dogs, even 1/4 mile away, had smelled the scent of a stranger, a north breeze blowing.

He was exhausted and seconds away from dieing. Later, Lorenzo's mother explained, "They came into our bedroom, grabbed me, put a pillow over my head with a gun pressing against me." Lorenzo's mother was recovering from her surgery and was at a loss for words.

Who could've done such an evil act? Why would someone want to hurt Lorenzo's parents?

Lorenzo was in shock, angry, scared and lost. He felt as if this was a bad dream, however it was reality.

Even though Lorenzo's parents were physically and emotionally distraught, they were still alive. Lorenzo thanked God for that. During the next hours, the sheriffs were doing investigations and taking fingerprints.

The weeks passed, then months, still no lead on who could have committed such a wicked act. Lorenzo would go to work each day puzzled and confused.

SEARCHING FOR THE TRUTH

Lorenzo knew friends that were not the most trusted and were on the streets. Maybe they would have some knowledge and are willing to talk. It is possible they might know… however, no one was talking. Lorenzo's father posted in the local newspaper a reward.

Lorenzo also made signs and posted them throughout the small town. Anyone with information leading to the arrest and conviction of the horrific act that had been cast upon his family.

The home invasion had left Lorenzo's family devastated. It was like an earthquake had hit, everyone was disoriented.

Lorenzo's mother became very anxious. Even though she was a strong woman, it affected her tremendously. His father was uneasy, he had broken ribs and his eyes were both swollen and black and blue. Lorenzo's friends would say, "Your father is such a strong man, it's hard for me to see him in this condition, this black cloud had rained upon the family."

Lorenzo was also worried and scared, not sleeping well. The family would install alarm systems, Lorenzo would sleep with his dogs nearby and also weapons at close reach. Lorenzo would wake up to any little movement. Lorenzo's wife, Jerry Ann, was concerned for her son, Santo. The tragic event had changed Lorenzo's family on that cold foggy windy night for the rest of his life until today…

EVALUATE

Lorenzo stopped and took a look at who he was associating with. Lorenzo was determined to bring these people forward and have them pay for what had occurred. Lorenzo always said… *it must be someone we know…* yet it never happened. No justice was served to his family.

Years later, an old friend came to Lorenzo. He asked if Lorenzo heard Elk had died. Lorenzo knew Elk died, yet was not a friend… Elk was a thug, a bully, and a loser. People like Elk prey on the weak. Karma is harsh. Elk will pay to someone. Lorenzo wondered why Dennis was bringing this up.

In fact, Lorenzo had known this person all his life. Dennis stated, "Yes, he died." Lorenzo had nothing to say because he did not like this bully that died. Dennis went on to tell Lorenzo, he thought this loser could have been the one who committed the home invasion at Lorenzo's parents some 5 years ago..

Lorenzo was angry and stunned. He yelled back to Dennis, why would Dennis,who himself is a drifter, bring this up now?

Why wouldn't he, if he had insight, not have told Lorenzo before.

At this point, Lorenzo told himself he would never engage with Dennis again.

This was a person that once upon a time was a friend that Lorenzo laughed with. The writing was on the wall.

Now Lorenzo thought, if Dennis had known then others would have known. close friends or so called friends.Lorenzo went on to confront some of the friends that knew Elk. They all denied. "We know nothing Lorenzo…"

"The moral of this story, Blood," Lorenzo told his dog, "Be careful of the tule fog and always think long and hard with relationships…"

May Lorenzo's parents rest in peace

Lorenzo continues to live his life on the family's small farm. His dog, Blood, has died yet Lorenzo has another loyal dog at his side.

He is a happy and loving friend..

Love and take care of your family and animals..